DATE		

The Prancing Pony

Nursery Rhymes from Japan

adapted into English verse for children by CHARLOTTE B.

PRANCING PoNY

DeFOREST ::: *with "kusa-e" illustrations by* KEIKO HIDA

A WEATHERMARK EDITION

WALKER/WEATHERHILL, NEW YORK & TOKYO

First edition, 1967 (Japan), 1968 (U. S.)
Third printing, 1969

Published by John Weatherhill, Inc., of New York & Tokyo
with editorial offices at 7-6-13 Roppongi, Minato-ku, Tokyo
Distributed in the Far East by John Weatherhill, Inc.
and in the United States by Walker and Company
720 Fifth Avenue, New York, N. Y. 10019

LCC No. 68-15698

DEDICATION

THESE VERSES BELONG
TO THE CHILDREN OF JAPAN
AND IT IS THEY, NOT WE,
WHO NOW OFFER THEM
TO CHILDREN EVERYWHERE

Table of Contents

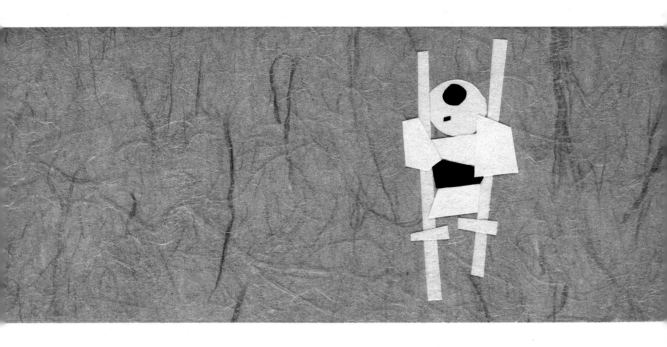

Publisher's Foreword

About the Rhymes. Rhymes should speak for themselves, and we hope
that those in this book are no exception. But the adult reader may wish
to know how the book came about. Briefly, the story is this:

The Reverend Tasuku Harada, one of Japan's outstanding Christian
educators, had a deep interest in nursery rhymes and gathered them
from all over Japan. By the turn of the century he had collected and
made literal translations of well over a hundred choice examples, and in
the early 1900's he asked Charlotte B. DeForest, who attended the Kobe
church of which he was then pastor, to put them into English verse.

Miss DeForest undertook this task with pleasure, and the resulting
manuscript was a joy to all who read it. A few of the verses were
published in the *Congregationalist* magazine at Boston in 1910, and some
more were included in a collection of Miss DeForest's poetry, *Poems
Down the Years*, published at Kobe in 1960. From time to time she
made revisions in her manuscript, but in the press of other matters she
never got around to publishing it. When the manuscript fortunately came
our way, we were immediately charmed by the rhymes and began making
plans to publish a selection of them for the wider audience they deserve.

But there was one further step. Miss DeForest had remained admirably

faithful to the originals, so much so that, given the differences in cultures and languages, her renderings were more for adult readers than for children. And yet, the same verses have delighted generations of Japanese children. So, at our suggestion, Miss DeForest undertook to recast her translations much more freely, to adapt them in thought forms and language that would evoke similar delight in children of other lands. In the process several of the editors dealing with the book—Meredith Weatherby, John Dower, Millicent Horton, and others—also enjoyed offering suggestions of their own, some of which Miss DeForest accepted, and some smilingly declined. And the reactions of a number of children to whom the verses were read also played a formative role.

The final versions that appear here, then, are adaptations in the best sense of the word, not literal translations. They are deft transmutations that we believe will appeal to children everywhere. They are also the product of much collaboration, but all bear the stamp of Miss DeForest's guiding hand.

And all, too, are faithful to their Japanese originals, in spirit and intent if not in word-for-word literalness. Rhyme and meter, neither of which are devices of Japanese verse, have been added, but with as little sacrifice of Japanese local color as possible. Sometimes English substitutes have been made for the onomatopoetic or nonsense words of the Japanese, although these too have been kept when they seemed self-explanatory. Sometimes concrete images have been used to explain things that might be unfamiliar to Western children.

Adult readers of the rhymes will at once recognize in them the Japanese characteristics of filial piety, industry, cooperativeness, and love of nature. A very few of the verses may perhaps have been composed by individual poets, but by and large they are spontaneous folk poetry, of anonymous authorship. Strictly speaking, some of them fall into the broader category of folk songs, for adults as well as for the young, but all have been enjoyed by children, and in this sense they all can be called nursery rhymes. Most are very old, though some are as recent as the present century. Some exist in many versions throughout Japan and are known to almost all Japanese, while others appear to be unique and regional. Many of them are still popular today. They are the words of lullabies and other songs that were sung to and by children, some having well-known melodies, while others were merely crooned by mothers and nursemaids to improvised tunes. As a part of Japanese folklore they grew out of daily-life experiences and, in their own simple way, are very much a reflection of Japanese folkways and folk wisdom.

Tasuku Harada, the collector, died in 1940. A graduate of Yale University's School of Theology, he served as president of Doshisha University, in Kyoto, and later as head of Japanese studies at the University of Hawaii. His son, the Honorable Ken Harada, of the Imperial Household Bureau, has generously given Miss DeForest permission for the present use of his father's collected material.

Charlotte B. DeForest was born in Japan of missionary parents, spent most of her life there, and knows its language and people well. After

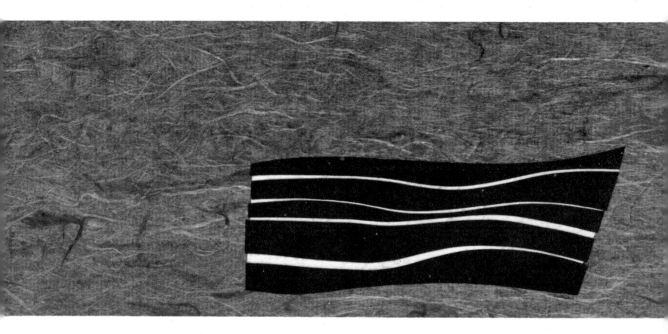

graduating from Smith College, she returned to Japan as a Congregational missionary and educator. For more than forty years her interest centered in Japan's well-known school for women, Kobe College, which she served as president for a quarter of a century. During her years there she also received two graduate degrees from Smith College and several awards from the Japanese government for her long educational service. She retired in 1950 and now makes her home in California, where she is still active at the age of eighty-eight. She is fondly remembered by her many former students, and the enthusiastic support of the Kobe College Alumnae Association has done much to make possible the publication of this book.

About the Illustrations.   Keiko Hida is one of Japan's most original and gifted artists. One has only to see her collages to remember always their frolicking children, their elegant ladies and magical landscapes, all depicted in inimitably gay and yet subtle colors. No wonder then that, above all others, she was the artist we wanted to illustrate this book. When we approached her with the idea, she accepted enthusiastically, and immediately set about snipping and tearing and cutting and pasting to create the illustrations that appear here. Clearly, her heart yet retains something of a child's vision and she still delights in nursery rhymes, particularly in rhymes such as these, many of which were among her childhood favorites. It was with a sense of wonder and enchantment that we watched worlds of fantasy take shape beneath her flying fingers.

For centuries the Japanese have loved playing with paper, sometimes folding it into charming creations called *origami* and sometimes pasting it into collage designs called *hari-e*. But it was the genius of Miss Hida that raised such paper play to the level of an art. She calls this new art *kusa-e*, and the name does much to explain the uniqueness of her inspiration. The term is made up of two words: *e*, meaning "picture," and *kusa*, with the basic meaning of "grass" and a wider artistic meaning that was first used to describe the free-flowing, elegant, cursive style often found in Japanese calligraphy. It was these same qualities Miss Hida wanted to capture in her collages—flowing grace, subtlety of form, abbreviation, simplicity, imagination. How well she has succeeded!

Look, for example, at the scroll of children she has created for the opening pages of this book. With what simple abbreviations are the children depicted, and yet how real and comprehensible they are. Often lacking essential facial features, and with bodies made of simple geometrical shapes, still to us they are dancing and running and singing, gesturing and pointing, smiling and crying. Even those in black and white and gray are still somehow filled with the colors of childhood. Miss Hida has given us in shorthand the essence of the child, intentionally leaving us to supply the details. And if we adults can see all this, how much more will the freer imagination of children be able to see? A number of the rhymes have been left unillustrated in the belief that some children will want to make their own collage illustrations for them.

Note, too, that Miss Hida never uses patterned paper in her collages:

the patterns also are to be filled in by the viewer's imagination. She tells the story of a man who came to her at one of her exhibitions and asked her to re-create for him one of her *kusa-e* that he had seen several years before. He said it was of a Japanese woman and he described in detail the pattern of her kimono. Miss Hida remembered the picture he had in mind, but she also knew there was no pattern in the woman's kimono. She was delighted with what the man had seen in her picture and felt sure she had thus created a more beautiful pattern in the man's imagination than could ever actually be seen.

The basic meaning of *kusa*—"grass" or "plant"—is also connected with Miss Hida's art. For only natural plant dyes are used to color the papers of her collages. The red comes from madder roots, brown from cedar bark and leaves, black from persimmon juice, indigo from the plant of that name, yellow from fruit of the cape jasmine, purple from wood of the Judas tree—truly a sorcerer's collection of colors. These colors are used to dye thin, beautifully textured, and surprisingly strong handmade Japanese paper, the kind that is often called rice paper in the West; it is made in the countryside by craftsmen using the same methods as those of many centuries past.

Keiko Hida was born at Osaka in 1913. Even as a child she was keenly aware of beauty. Once she went into the country to look at the cherry blossoms. A sudden wind came up and she was caught in a rain of cherry petals. Returning home, she cried into the night, remembering not only the beauty of the blossoms but the poignancy of their falling

This incident she recalled while doing the illustration for "The Prancing Pony," the title poem of this book.

Her versatile artistry has many facets. She began her career as a teacher of classical Japanese dance. After the war she went into the seclusion of a Buddhist nunnery for five years. Now, besides her wide *kusa-e* activities, she writes poetry and essays and is well known for her exquisite calligraphy, which she sometimes brushes on her collages. She is also an accomplished photographer and kimono designer. Several thousands of students have studied at her Tokyo *kusa-e* school, but her art is by no means limited to Japan alone. She is an enthusiastic traveler and has visited Europe and the Americas each year since 1961. She has many overseas students, both adult and young, particularly in New York, Los Angeles, and Rome. Over 400,000 copies of a how-to-do-it booklet she has prepared in English will shortly be distributed to school children in California, where the rudiments of *kusa-e* are being taught in many grade schools. And her numerous exhibitions and lectures, both at home and abroad, are constantly winning her even more admirers. We are proud to present her here to another audience.

The Prancing Pony

Sleepy Sparrows

Wake up, little sparrows,
    And open your eyes;
Come sit on a twig,
    And see the sun rise.

Come out of your soft
    Sleepy nest in the tree,
And play, little sparrows,
    And sing for me.

The Barefoot Bat

Barefooted bat,
    Come down from the sky,
        And I'll give you some clogs to wear.

Poor little bat,
    For you I will buy
        A beautiful, brand-new pair.

The Penniless Hawk

O hawk in the sky there—
    Sing to-ro-ro—
        Please drop me a penny down.

Or if you've no money—
    Sing to-ro-ro—
        Then drop me a feather brown.

Good and Bad

Yesterday you didn't like me;
    I was naughty then.
But today you like me, don't you?
    I am good again.

A Flower Lullaby

Lul-la, lul-la, lullaby,
Pretty baby, sleep, don't cry.

Where has Baby's
   mother gone,
Where, oh where?
Picking flowers
   in the hills,
Up there, up there.

One she picks,
   and two she picks,
And puts them in her gown.

But when she picks
   the third one,
The sun goes down.

When will baby's
   mother come,
When, oh when?
Soon she'll come,
   she's almost home,
And then, and then—

Lul-la, lul-la, lullaby,
Pretty baby, sleep, don't cry.

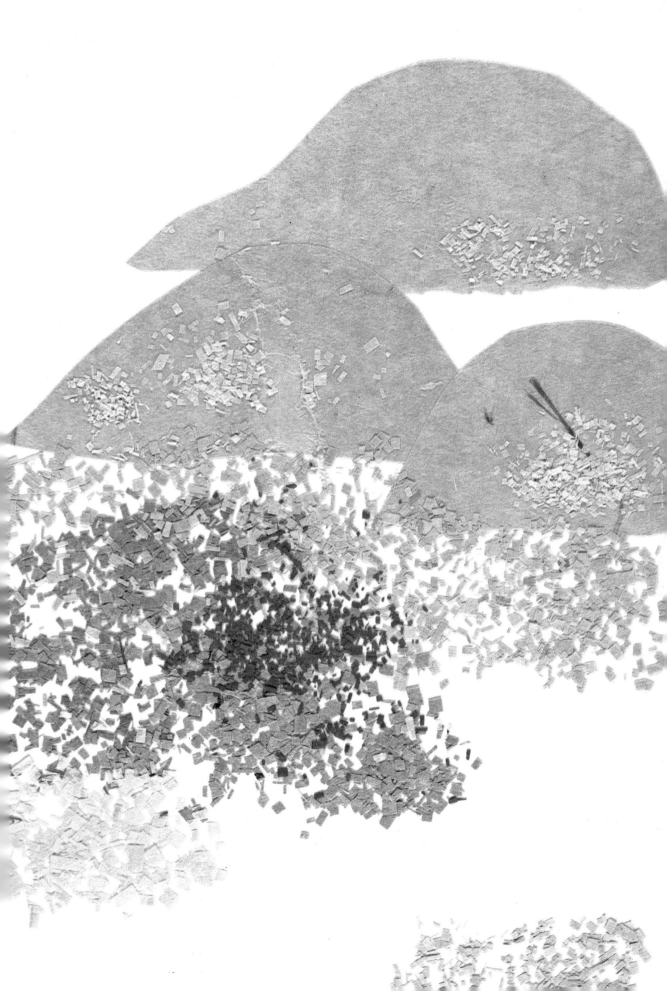

Little Miss Moon

Little Miss Moon,
Pretty Miss Moon,
How old are you tonight?

What, only seven?
Not yet eleven?
How young to be so bright!

Gifts for a Good Boy

Now if you're good while I'm away—
Tum, tum, tum,
A deer-skin drum—
I'll bring you gifts this very day—
Toot, toot, toot,
A bamboo flute.

The Millstream

Round goes the mill,
And down the hill
The water flows and flows.
We sleep at night,
But dark or light
On and on it goes.

Twins

Two little girls were standing there.
They'd combed alike their long black hair;
Their bright kimono were the same.
They asked us to a guessing game:
They said to us, "We're sisters, yes,
But which is older? You must guess."

Sparrows or Butterflies?

A sparrow's on a willow twig.
What's he doing?
He's dancing a jig.

> A butterfly is on a rose.
> And what's *he* doing?
> He's waving his nose.

>> Now, which is prettier, tell me true?
>> Why, sparrows are — and butterflies too.

Three Seagulls

Here on this bridge let's sit on the railing
    And look far out to sea;
High in the air three seagulls are sailing,
    Happy as can be.

Where Do Rivers Go?

"Where does a river hurry so?"
"Drop in your cap, and then you'll know:
Straight to the sea—that's where it will go."

A Question

I asked a seagull on the bay,
"When does the tide come in today?"

"I'm only a wandering bird," it said;
"You'll have to ask the waves instead."

Falling Snow

Snow is falling, falling hard—
        Kon-ko, kon-ko, ko.
Falling in the temple yard—
        Kon-ko, kon-ko, ko.
See the big persimmon tree
Turning white as white can be—
        Kon—kon—ko.

Weeping Cherry Trees

Beside the Bay
    of Okura
The weeping cherry
    trees hang low.
Let's gather branches
    bright with blooms—
Do come with me!
    Oh, please let's go!

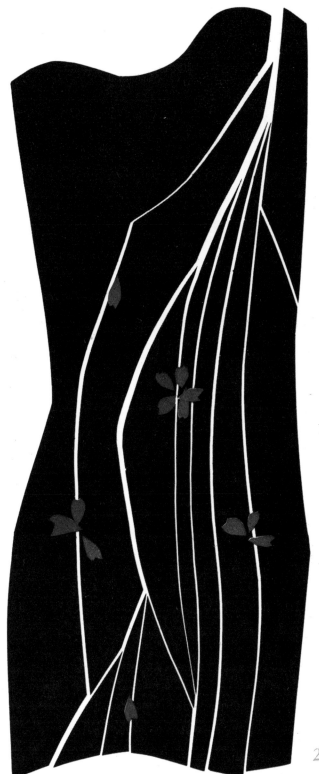

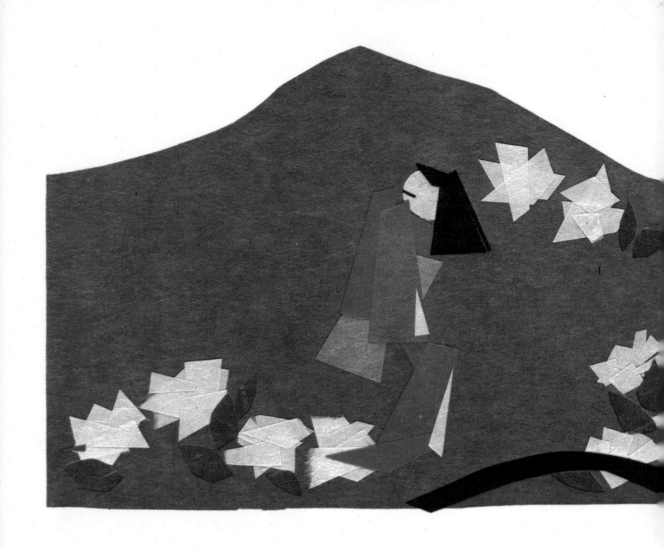

Thorn Song

I was walking there along the hill
When a wild rose caught and held me still.
"You thorns," I said, "don't hold me so:
It's getting dark and I must go."

Long-nosed Elf

Elf, elf, long-nosed elf,
   It's so hot today.
From, from, from the sky
   Send a breeze my way.

If, if, if you have
   Not a single breeze,
Then, then, then I want
   A penny if you please.

The Prancing Pony

Your prancing, dancing pony—
    Oh, please don't tie him here.
This cherry tree's in blossom—
    Oh, dear, dear, dear!

He'll prance and dance and whinny,
    He'll neigh and stamp and call,
And down the soft, pink blossoms
    Will fall, fall, fall!

Snowman

Quilly-quo,
A quart of snow.
Pilly-pail,
A pint of hail.
Oh, see the snowflakes fall!

Tilly-toll,
The snowballs roll
To make a snowman tall!

With charcoal eyes,
He looks so wise—
And thinks he knows it all!

Chrysanthemum Colors

By the garden fence chrysanthemums grow.
Let's count the colors in the row:
There's white and yellow and then there's red,
All blooming in our chrysanthemum bed.

Seven Gifts

It's seven incense boxes
    For the boy who quiet lies;
But seven heavy stones
    If he stays awake and cries.

To See a Nightingale

A nightingale's singing—
    Come quick, let's go see.
But wait! If you're barefoot
    You shan't come with me.

An April Child

A baby born in April
    Is like—what do you think?—
Is like a cherry blossom,
    Sweet and round and pink.

Catching Dragonflies

Dragonflies, hey!
Dragonflies, say!
Do stop a minute there!
Catch you I will!
Grab you I will!
And then I'll put you—where?

A Round Trip

Little bat, quick little bat,
    Down to the meadow fly.
Touch the grasses with your wing;
    Then fly back to the sky.
    Fly back to the sky.

A Warning to Crows

O crows, take care! beware!
    Do keep a sharp lookout!
A hunter with a gun
    Is looking about.

The Spinners

Spin, spin, spin—
You are spinning silk for kings
Spin, spin, spin—
I spin hemp for bridle strings.

The Tea Roaster

Hey, little dog, don't bark at me!
I'm not a beggar, can't you see?
In that shop there I roast the tea
Till it tastes good as tea can be.

Town and Country

In town you have expensive clocks
    To tell the time of day;
But here we have a nightingale
    To say spring's on its way.

Wild Geese Flying

Look how the wild geese fly and fly,
Tiny black dots in the moonlit sky.
Behind the old ones the youngsters come—
I wonder where they started from.

Two Puppies

Whitie, come fast,
    Catch a cake for a treat!
Blackie, come quick,
    Catch a rice-ball to eat!

First you say, "Thank you,"
    And then you may go.
Round about, round about! . . .
    Don't be so slow!

A Cat Called Little Bell

Kitty, kitty, pretty thing —
Ting-a-ling a-ling a-ling.
    Around your neck a little bell
Goes ting-a-ling a-ling a-ling.
    That's why we call you Little Bell,
Kitty, kitty, pretty thing.

Getting-up Time

Wake up, wake up, you sleepyhead!
　　The crows have taken wing.
Wake up, wake up, get out of bed!
　　Just hear the sparrows sing.

Wind Message

The wind is blowing, blowing, blowing
　　Here and there;
The wind is going, going, going
　　Everywhere.

North Wind, I wish you'd talk,
　　I wish you had a mouth
To say for me "Good morning"
　　To my friends there in the south.

A Ghost Story

"Hello, you, are you a ghost,
Hiding there behind that post?"

"No, I'm just an old dead tree—
You needn't be afraid of me."

A Hunted Deer

Hear from the forest the cry of a deer!
She's cold, or she's lost, or she's hungry, I fear.

No, none of those things; it's because they have found her,
And forty-four hunters are closing around her.

Mountains on Mountains

"Look over there
        And what do you see?"
"Mountains and mountains—
        That's what I see."

"Look over here
        And what do you see?"
"Mountains, more mountains—
        That's all I can see."

"But there in those mountains
        Is there nothing at all?"
                "Yes, acorns, and berries,
                        And nuts—that's all."

A Winter's Dream

In an old plum tree
A nightingale nods,
    Cold as cold can be.
He dreams a dream
Of flowers in spring
    Blooming merrily.

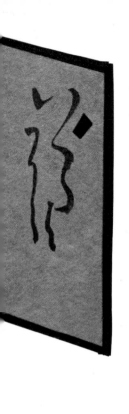

A Dream Party

Lullaby, lullaby, slumberland bound,
When our baby's sleeping sound,
We'll go out and buy a fish
And call our friends to share the dish.
And when they ask what feast we're keeping,
We'll say, "The feast of Baby's sleeping."

Lullaby, lullaby, slumberland bound,
Please sleep soon and please sleep sound;
And in your dreams you're sure to see
A finer feast than ours will be.

The Song of the Frog

So hushaby, baby, if you'll go to sleep,
I'll give you a pretty red flower to keep.
But if you keep crying, a big ugly frog
Will croak by your side—kerchog! kerchog!

The Frogs' Call

The frogs in the pond are calling, calling:
        "Kwa,
                Kwa,
                        Kwa!"
Ask what they mean, and they answer you bawling:
        "Kwa,
                Kwa,
                        Kwa!"

Why Rabbits Jump

"Why are you rabbits jumping so?
    Now please tell why, tell why."
"We jump to see the big round moon
    Up in the sky, the sky."

The Lonely Boy

I see a temple through the trees;
    It is a lonely view.
There stands a little temple boy—
    And he is lonely too.

The Fisherman

On the open sea off Hiburi
My father's fishing for salmon trout,
And waves are tossing his boat about.

Rain Riddle

Sometimes the rain falls straight,
    Sometimes it slants and dives.
        Now why? why? why?

Sometimes the wind is still,
    Sometimes it blows and drives.
        That's why! why! why!

Pigeon Playmates

You pigeons on the temple roof,
Please fly down here with a poof-poof-poof,
    And a pop-po, pop-po!
Come eat the beans I have for you,
And don't go back when you get through,
But stay and play, with a coo-coo-coo,
    And a pop-po, pop-po!

55

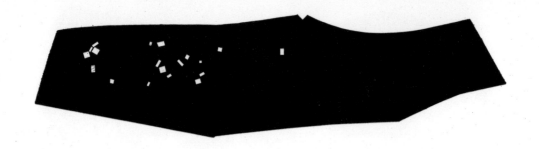

A Lost Snowflake

The snowflakes fell, the first this year.
I caught one on my sleeve—right here!
I thought that we would play all day.
But then it melted—right away!

Flower Song

Just see what's opened up today!
 What flowers are they?
 What flowers are they?
They're peonies, so people say.
Our peonies have bloomed today!

Just see what's folded up tonight!
 What flowers are they?
 What flowers are they?
They're lotus flowers, all creamy-white.
Our lotus flowers have shut up tight!

Morning-glories

How bravely morning-glory vines
 Go climbing toward the light!
They twine about a bamboo fence
 And hold on, oh, so tight.

In the Spring

 Let's go, let's go!
 It's spring you know.
The fields are sparkling bright
 With violets blue,
 Dandelions too.
It's such a lovely sight!

Light for a Bride

A light shines bright,
    Now here, now there.
The moon?   A star
    Far off somewhere?

No, it's a torch
    To light the bride
Who's coming down
    The mountainside.

Two Birds Flying

Two birds were flying,
    One behind, one ahead.
They changed places,
    And instead, and instead—
The one behind
    Was ahead, was ahead.

Firefly Party

O fireflies dear,
Come to the feast
That's waiting for you here.

It's a feast of dew
Spread on the grass
Especially for you.

The "weathermark" identifies this book as having been designed and produced at John Weatherhill, Inc., 6-13, Roppongi 7-chome, Minato-ku, Tokyo / Book design, typography & layout by Meredith Weatherby / Composition, engraving & printing by Toppan, Tokyo / Binding by Makoto Binderies, Tokyo / The typeface used throughout is hand-set Goudy Bold, with the verses in 14 point and the introduction in 12 point